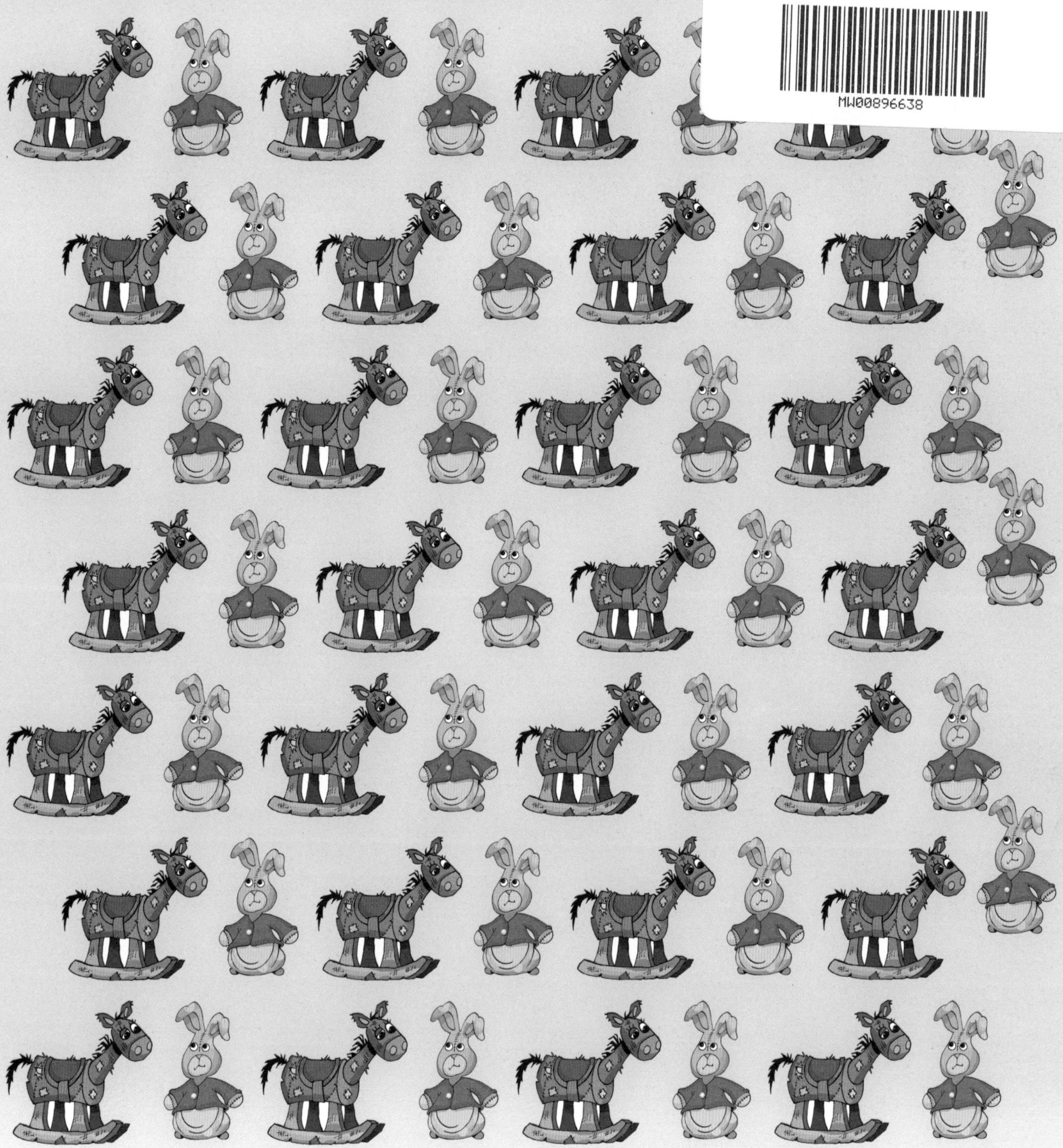

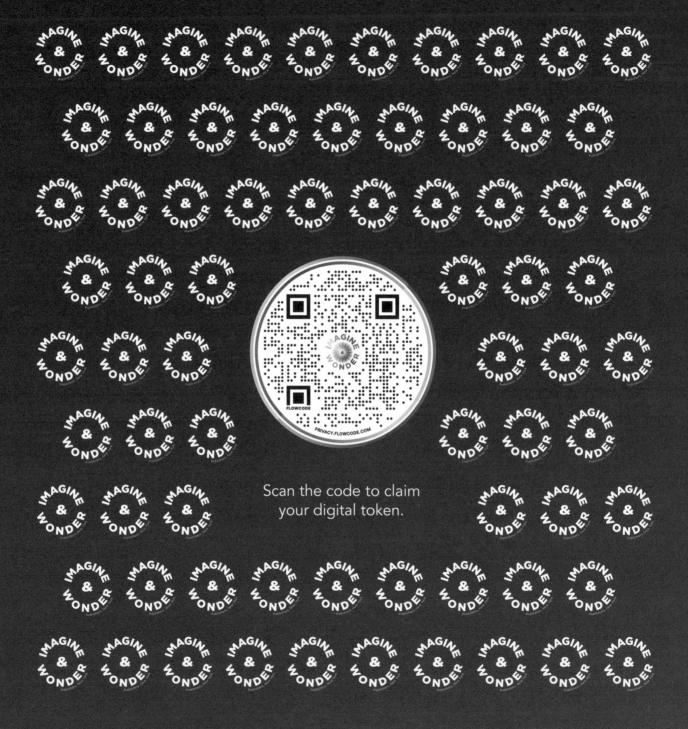

Scan the code to claim
your digital token.

THIS BOOK BELONGS TO:

THE Velveteen Rabbit

Donald Kasen and David Van Hooser

Scan this QR code with your phone camera
for more titles from imagine and wonder

Your guarantee of quality
As publishers, we strive to produce every book to the highest commercial standards.
The printing and binding have been planned to ensure a sturdy, attractive publication
which should give years of enjoyment. If your copy fails to meet our high standards,
please inform us and we will gladly replace it. admin@imagineandwonder.com

The Velveteen Rabbit first appeared on a Christmas morning. He was peeking from over the top of the Boy's stocking hanging over the fireplace. Just enough for someone to see his thread whiskers, nose and pink satin ears. The rest of his chubby brown and white spotted body, which was dressed in a blue jacket, was nestled into the stocking along with small trinkets, candy and other treats.

In the company of so many other toys that seemed more colorful and exciting, the Velveteen Rabbit was soon all but forgotten. He was shy, and was sometimes made fun of by other toys who saw him as nothing more than a stuffed bunny.

The only one really kind to the Rabbit was the Skin Horse. He was the oldest of all the toys. His brown coat was bald in spots. His seams showed and threads were loose. His hair was thin. Yet, he was very wise, and understood how Magic worked among toys.

The Rabbit asked him, “What is REAL? I’ve heard the word spoken a lot by other toys.”

“Real is a thing when a toy has spent a long time becoming a child’s true friend,” said the Skin Horse. “When a child really cares for you, not just to play with but love you from the heart, then you become Real.”

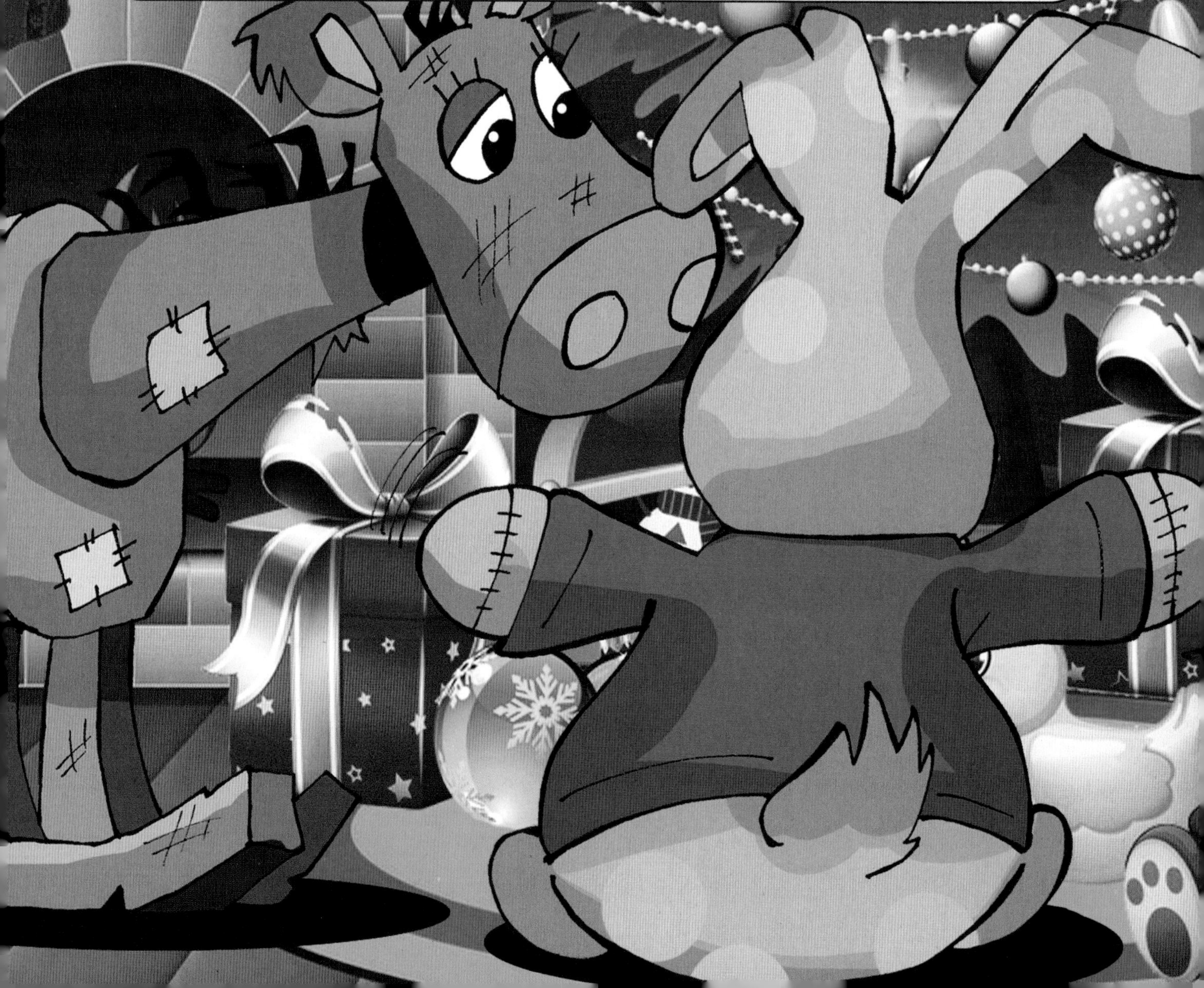

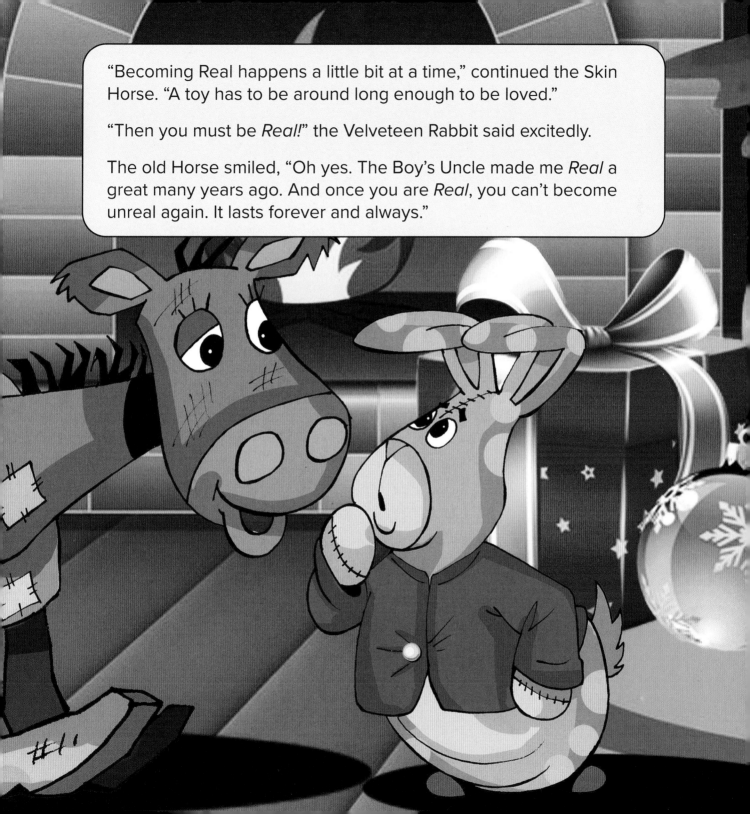

"Becoming Real happens a little bit at a time," continued the Skin Horse. "A toy has to be around long enough to be loved."

"Then you must be *Real!*" the Velveteen Rabbit said excitedly.

The old Horse smiled, "Oh yes. The Boy's Uncle made me *Real* a great many years ago. And once you are *Real*, you can't become unreal again. It lasts forever and always."

That gave the Rabbit much to think about, much to hope for.

"*Real*... will I ever become *Real*? Will the little Boy ever, ever love me enough for that to happen?"

As if in answer to the Rabbit's hopes, the night came when the Boy couldn't find the teddy bear he usually slept with. The child's Grandmother scooped the Velveteen Rabbit from the floor and placed him next to the Boy in bed. "Here you go. Your bunny will make a good sleep mate for you."

That night, and for many nights after, the Velveteen Rabbit slept in the Boy's bed. At first, the Rabbit wasn't sure he really liked this. Because sometimes the Boy hugged him very tight and would roll over on him. That would make it hard for the Rabbit to breathe.

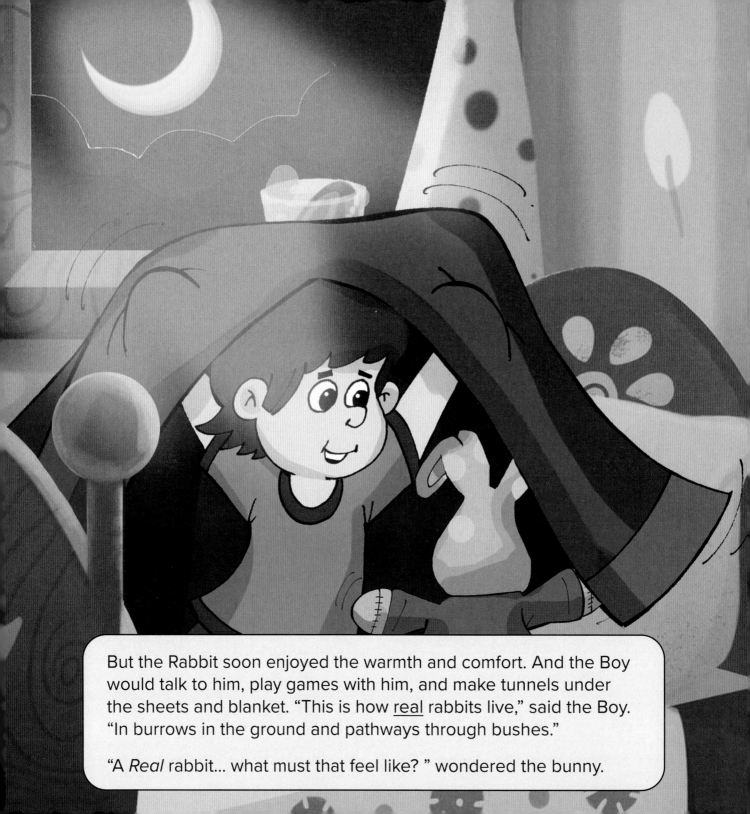

But the Rabbit soon enjoyed the warmth and comfort. And the Boy would talk to him, play games with him, and make tunnels under the sheets and blanket. "This is how <u>real</u> rabbits live," said the Boy. "In burrows in the ground and pathways through bushes."

"A *Real* rabbit... what must that feel like? " wondered the bunny.

As time went on, the little Rabbit was very happy! So happy that he didn't even notice how his beautiful velveteen fur was getting shabby and his jacket becoming worn. He wasn't aware that his tail was coming unsewn and the pink was rubbing off his nose because the Boy kissed him so much.

What was happening became clearer to the Velveteen Rabbit on one Spring day when the Boy took him outside. The Boy tossed him in the air and caught him softly, showed him the garden and woods, then had a picnic with cookies and a carrot (which the bunny had no idea what to do with).

When the Boy was called into the house later, he forgot to take the Rabbit. So the bunny sat outside until it got dark. Finally, the Grandmother showed up to get him. "There you are, you rascal. Do you know my grandson says he can't sleep without you?"

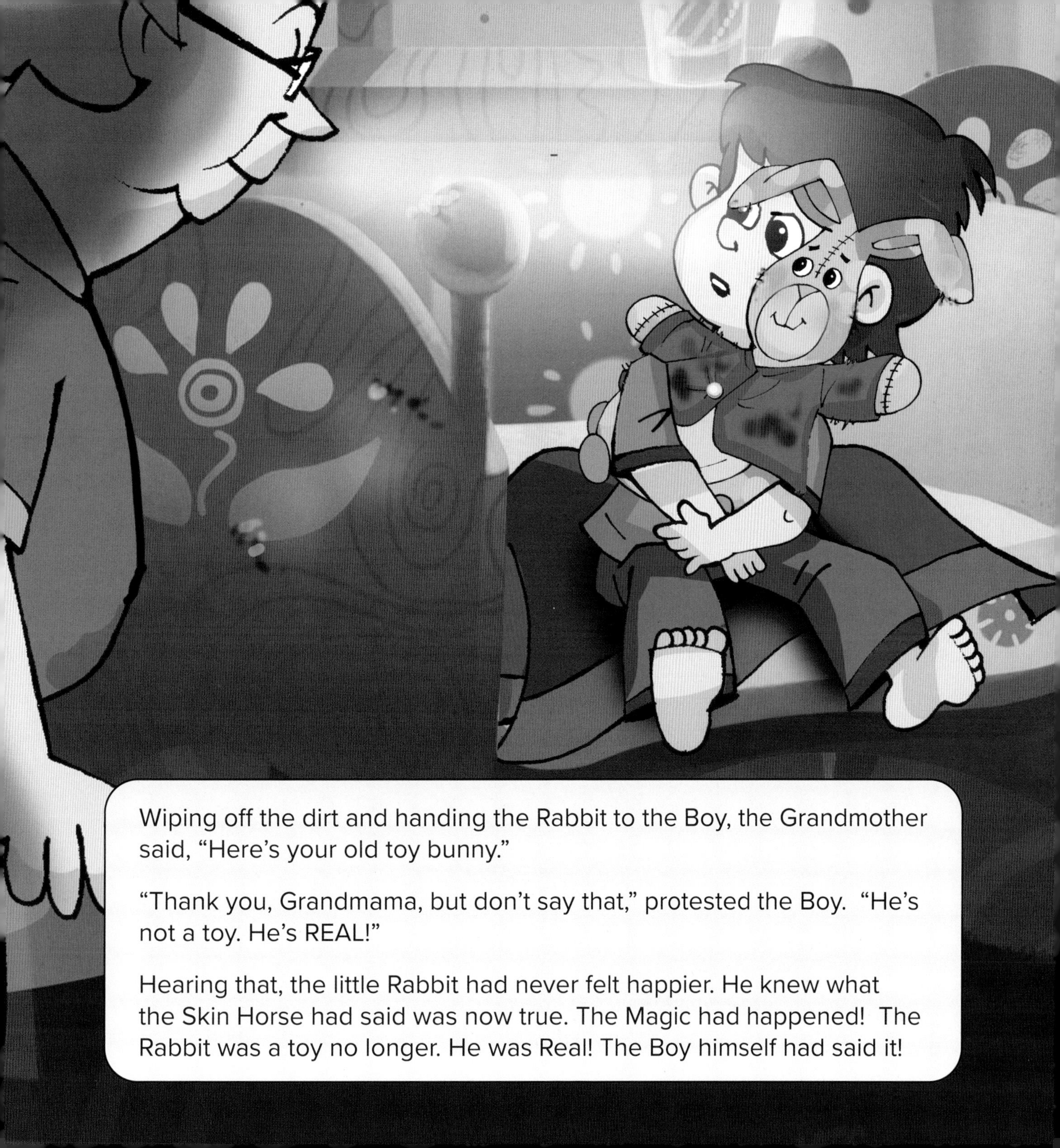

Wiping off the dirt and handing the Rabbit to the Boy, the Grandmother said, “Here’s your old toy bunny.”

“Thank you, Grandmama, but don’t say that,” protested the Boy. “He’s not a toy. He’s REAL!”

Hearing that, the little Rabbit had never felt happier. He knew what the Skin Horse had said was now true. The Magic had happened! The Rabbit was a toy no longer. He was Real! The Boy himself had said it!

The Summer that followed was wonderful. One day the Boy took the Rabbit to the edge of the garden. He pulled blades of grass to make a comfortable nest for his bunny, then the Boy wandered to a field to pick wild flowers that were in full bloom.

As the Velveteen Rabbit enjoyed a cool breeze, he saw two strange creatures appear from a bush. They were rabbits like himself, but looked furry and new. There were no seams or loose threads. And they didn't stay the same shape; going from long and thin to fat and bunchy when they moved.

They came closer. "What's that thing you're wearing? And why don't you jump up and play with us?" asked one bunny.

"Cause I don't want to," replied the Rabbit abruptly.

"Like this," shouted the furry bunny as he hopped up on his hind legs.

The two rabbits hopped nearer. One stretched out to look closer. "Why, he doesn't have any hind legs at all! Fancy a rabbit with no hind legs to jump with!"

"Jump up and dance," said the other rabbit.

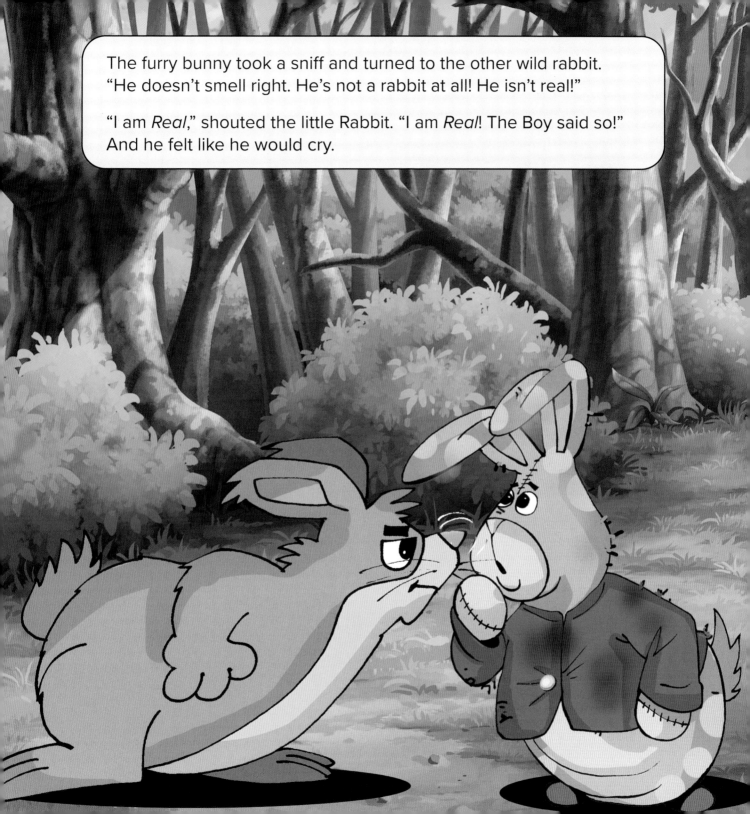

The furry bunny took a sniff and turned to the other wild rabbit. "He doesn't smell right. He's not a rabbit at all! He isn't real!"

"I am *Real*," shouted the little Rabbit. "I am *Real*! The Boy said so!" And he felt like he would cry.

Just then the Boy came running back which made the two strange rabbits scamper away.

"Please come back and play," called the Velveteen Rabbit. "I know I am *Real*." But the wild bunnies did not return.

As weeks passed, the little Rabbit grew very old and shabby, but the Boy loved him just as much and thought he was beautiful. That's all that mattered to the Rabbit. He knew the Magic had made him *Real*, and when you are *Real*, how you look doesn't matter.

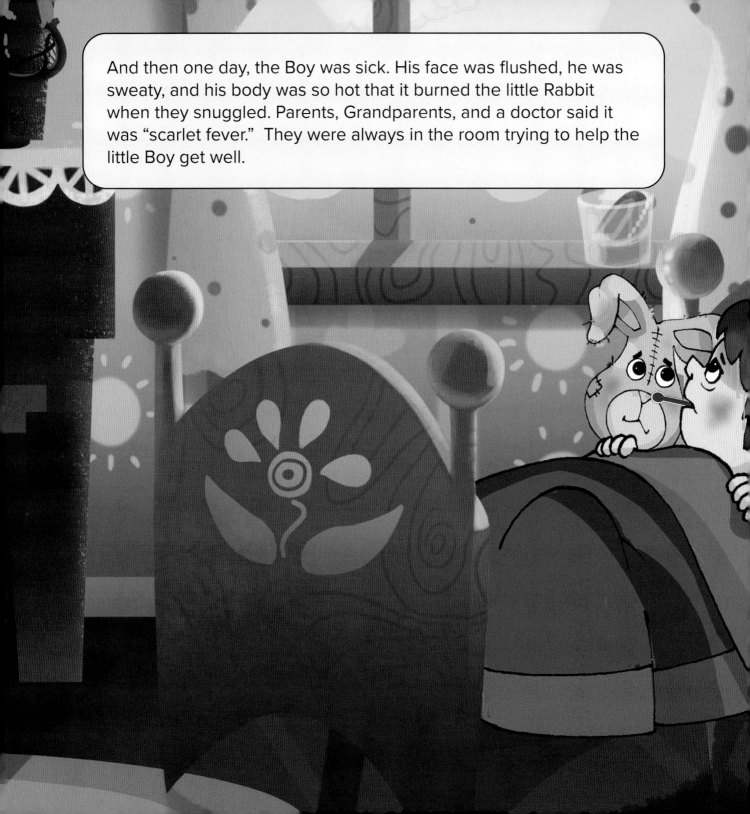

And then one day, the Boy was sick. His face was flushed, he was sweaty, and his body was so hot that it burned the little Rabbit when they snuggled. Parents, Grandparents, and a doctor said it was "scarlet fever." They were always in the room trying to help the little Boy get well.

The Velveteen Rabbit stayed in bed close to the Boy's side. He waited for the Boy to get better so they could go outside and play again. As the Boy slept, the little Rabbit would whisper into his ear about all the fun things they would do once the Boy became well.

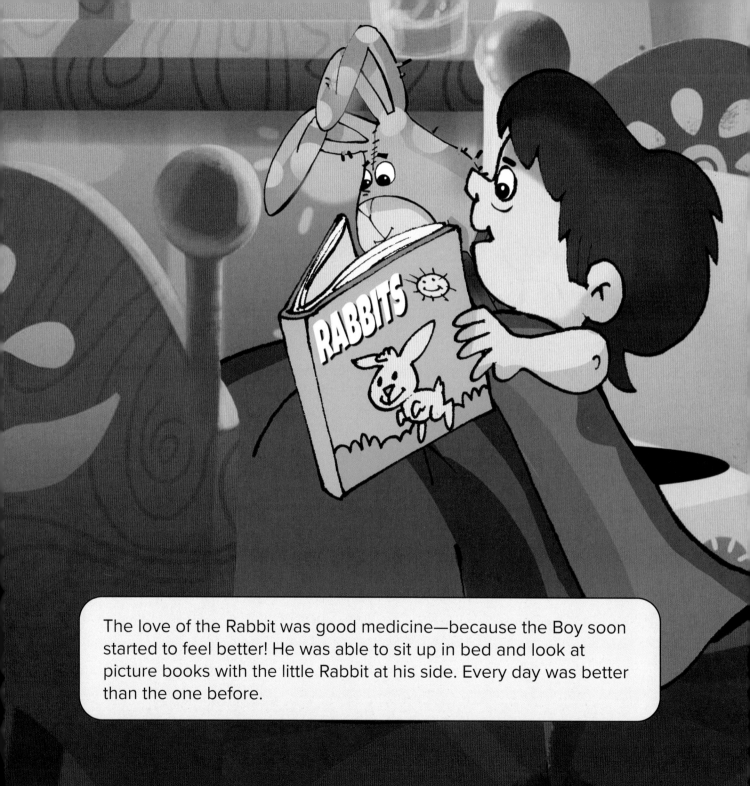

The love of the Rabbit was good medicine—because the Boy soon started to feel better! He was able to sit up in bed and look at picture books with the little Rabbit at his side. Every day was better than the one before.

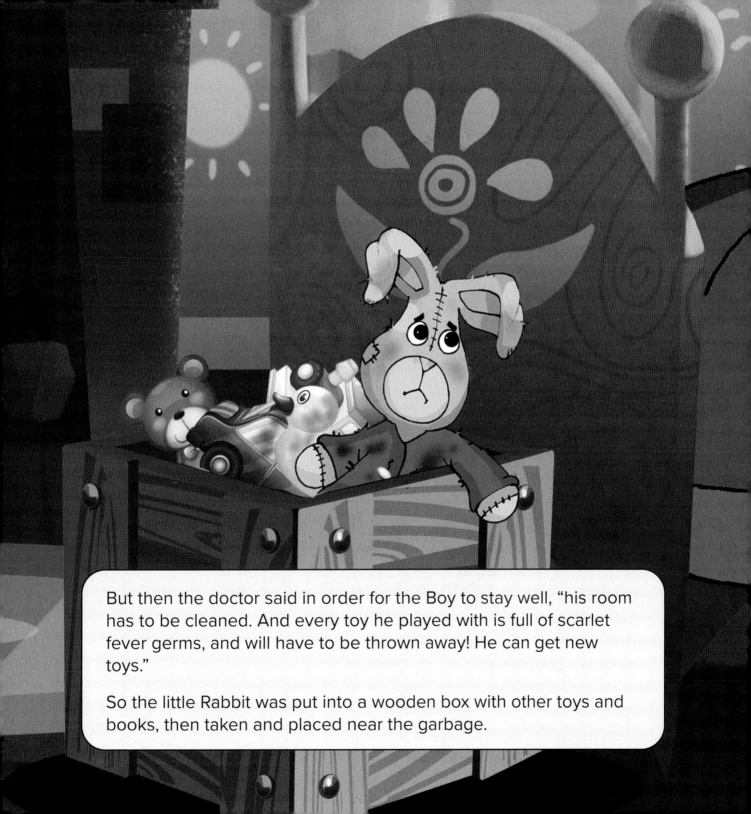

But then the doctor said in order for the Boy to stay well, "his room has to be cleaned. And every toy he played with is full of scarlet fever germs, and will have to be thrown away! He can get new toys."

So the little Rabbit was put into a wooden box with other toys and books, then taken and placed near the garbage.

Night came. The little Rabbit poked his head out of the box, knowing the next day that he and the other toys would be thrown away. He thought about the times he and the Boy cuddled and played together. And a tear, a _real_ tear, trickled down his shabby velvet nose and fell to the ground.

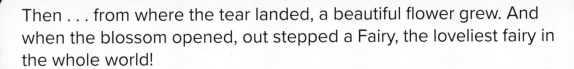

Then . . . from where the tear landed, a beautiful flower grew. And when the blossom opened, out stepped a Fairy, the loveliest fairy in the whole world!

"Little Rabbit," she said, "I am the Magic Fairy of all the playthings children have loved. I take the toys with me and turn them into *Real*."

But I'm already Real!" said the Rabbit.

"You were Real to the Boy because he loved you very much," said the Fairy. Tonight I will make you Real to everyone."

She gently kissed the Rabbit on the nose. "Now you shall become Real to all." With that, they rose and flew away.

They landed in a village of wild rabbits. The Fairy gathered them close. "I've brought you a new playmate. Be kind and teach him all he needs to know. He is going to live with you forever and ever!"

The other rabbits hopped up on their legs and began to dance. But the little Rabbit just sat there.

Then the little Rabbit noticed that he now had the body and legs of a Real Rabbit! So he jumped high into the air. He twirled and danced with his new friends! His legs, his face, his nose, his whiskers—everything about him was new and *Real!*

Time passed and Spring came again. One day the little Boy went out to play in the woods. Out from a bush hopped a little rabbit with strange markings under his fur, as though he had once been spotted. The Boy looked closely at the creature's little nose and round black eyes.

"Why, he looks just like my old Bunny that was lost when I had scarlet fever!"

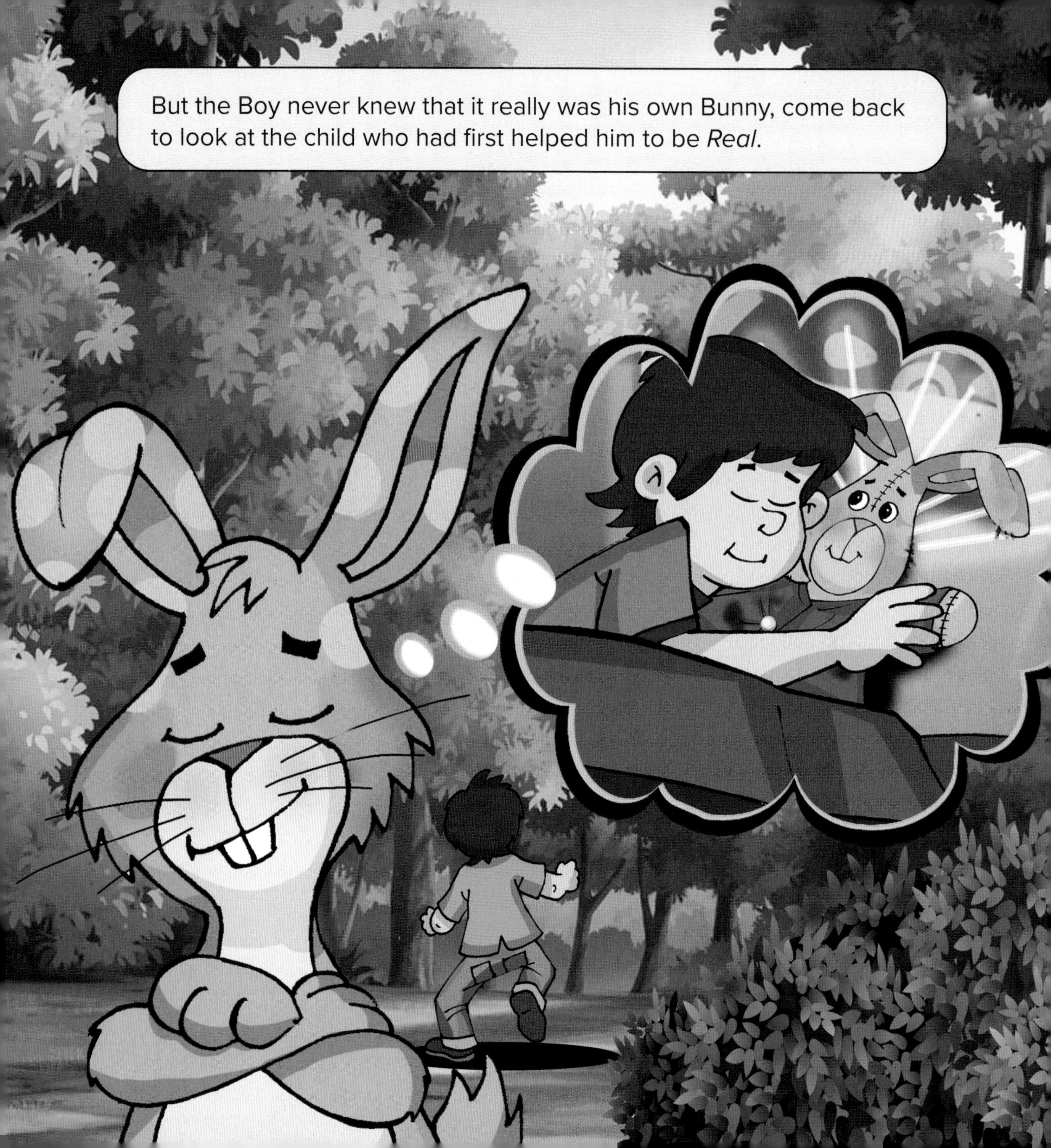
But the Boy never knew that it really was his own Bunny, come back to look at the child who had first helped him to be *Real*.

Scan the QR code to find other
amazing adventures and more from
www.ImagineAndWonder.com

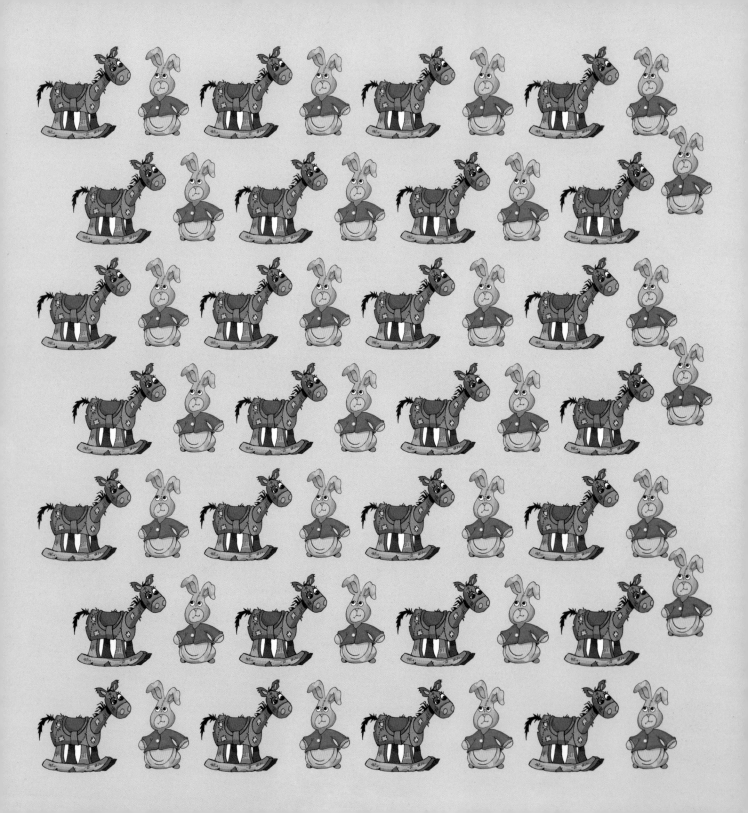